VALLEY 1/24/2007
506900105
LeBoutill
The story of the Seattle
Supersonics /

S0-GHT-443

VALLEY COMMUNITY LIBRARY
739 RIVER STREET
PECKVILLE, PA 18452
(570) 489-1765
www.lclshome.org

THE STORY OF THE
SEATTLE
SUPERSONICS

CREATIVE EDUCATION

Published by Creative Education
123 South Broad Street
Mankato, Minnesota 56001
Creative Education is an imprint of The Creative Company.

DESIGN AND PRODUCTION BY **EVANSDAY DESIGN**

PHOTOGRAPHS BY Getty Images (Anthony Potter Collection, Andrew D. Bernstein / NBAE, Chris Birck / NBAE, Dan Callister / NBAE, Jonathan Daniel, Tim Defrisco, George Gojkovich / NBAE, Otto Greule / Allsport, Otto Greule Jr. / NBAE, Elsa Hasch / NBAE, Andy Hayt / NBAE, Ron Hoskins / NBAE, Walter Iooss Jr. / NBAE, NBA Photo Library / NBAE, Anthony Neste / Mike Powell, NBAE, Wen Roberts / NBAE, Rick Stewart)

Copyright © 2007 Creative Education.
International copyright reserved in all countries.
No part of this book may be reproduced in any form
without written permission from the publisher.
Printed in the United States of America

LIBRARY OF CONGRESS CATALOGING-IN-PUBLICATION DATA

LeBoutillier, Nate.
The story of the Seattle Supersonics / by Nate LeBoutillier.
p. cm. — (The NBA—a history of hoops)
Includes index.
ISBN-13: 978-1-58341-425-5
1. Seattle Supersonics (Basketball team)—History—
Juvenile literature. I. Title. II. Series.

GV885.52.S4L43 2006
796.323'6409797772—dc22   2005051765

First edition

9 8 7 6 5 4 3 2 1

COVER PHOTO: *Ray Allen*

THE STORY OF THE SEATTLE SUPERSONICS

NATE LeBOUTILLIER

You get the ball

AND THINK YOU HAVE A CHANCE TO SHOOT IT, BUT HERE COMES THE SEATTLE SUPERSONICS' GARY PAYTON TO GUARD YOU. HE GETS CLOSER TO YOU THAN MOST DEFENDERS DARE, BECAUSE HE'S ULTRA-CONFIDENT IN HIS QUICK FEET AND HANDS. YOU DECIDE TO MAKE A BREAK FOR THE BASKET, BUT HE IS ALL OVER YOU, LIKE A GLOVE ON A HAND. YOU PICK UP YOUR DRIBBLE AND LOOK TO PASS…BUT PAYTON'S GREEN NUMBER 20 JERSEY SEEMS SUFFOCATING. SUDDENLY, HE PRIES THE BALL FROM YOU AND HEADS THE OTHER WAY DOWN THE COURT. YOU'RE ANOTHER VICTIM OF "THE GLOVE."

SONIC BEGINNINGS

SEATTLE, WASHINGTON, IS A CITY KNOWN FOR ITS large and impressive features. The 607-foot Space Needle, nearby snowcapped Mount Ranier, surrounding sprawling forests, and sparkling blue water of Puget Sound all impress with their size. Seattle is also home to the Boeing Company, which builds some of the world's largest jets. In 1967, Seattle added another high-flying attraction—a team in the National Basketball Association (NBA). Fittingly, the franchise was named in honor of the powerful jets, becoming the Seattle SuperSonics.

SEATTLE SUPERSONICS

Seattle's NBA team took its name from the local Boeing company's supersonic (faster-than-sound) jets

Although best known for his scoring prowess, All-Star Spencer Haywood was also a dominant rebounder.

The SuperSonics' first season ended with a 23–59 record. Forward Walt Hazzard provided plenty of offense, but the Sonics seemed to lack leadership. Seattle solved that problem after the season by trading Hazzard to the Atlanta Hawks for veteran guard Lenny Wilkens.

The trade paid off immediately. In 1968–69, Wilkens finished second in the NBA in assists as Seattle improved its record by seven wins. The next season, Wilkens became player-coach. His calm personality and intelligence made him a great coach, and his speed made him an All-Star player. In 1971–72, Seattle posted its first winning record.

Part of the reason for Seattle's improvement was Spencer Haywood, an explosive young forward known for his great shooting touch. "When Spencer was on, he could demoralize the other team single-handedly," explained Sonics center Bob Rule. "He'd pull up from 25 feet and launch one [shot] after another into the rafters. Somehow the ball would usually come down *snap* in the center of the basket."

THE NBA'S SLICK LOOK

Fashion trends come and go in the NBA, and one that has come, gone, and come back again is the headband. Don "Slick" Watts, a guard who played for the SuperSonics for five seasons in the mid-1970s, was one of the first to make headband-wearing fashionable, sporting it cockeyed on his bald head. "All these guys wearing headbands now are just following Slick Watts," said John Lucas, a former NBA guard and coach. "But he was more than a guy with a headband. He was a good point guard who really knew how to distribute the ball." Watts taught physical education in Seattle's schools following his NBA career. "It's good to see the kids come back with the headbands," Watts said. "It lets people know that Slick Watts is still alive."

With the Sonics on the rise, management traded Wilkens to Cleveland for young guard Butch Beard. The move backfired. Without Wilkens leading the way, the Sonics plummeted to 26–56 in 1972–73. To right the ship, Seattle then brought in former NBA star Bill Russell as coach.

In only his second season in Seattle, Russell guided the Sonics to a winning record and their first trip to the playoffs. Providing firepower during that 1974–75 season were Haywood and guard Fred Brown, whose long-range bombs earned him the nickname "Downtown Freddie Brown." Both players averaged more than 21 points per game.

The real spark plug that drove the Sonics, though, was Don "Slick" Watts. At a slim 6-foot-1, Watts was known for his great speed and quick hands—and the bright green headband he wore around his bald head. After arriving in 1973, Watts won over Seattle fans with his hustle and community involvement. "In the 10 years of the Sonics, I don't know of one player on a par with Slick Watts as far as desire on the court and ability to make people happy," team owner Sam Schulman once said. "I wish I had 12 Slick Wattses on my team."

SEATTLE SUPERSONICS

Fred Brown played 13 seasons in Seattle, setting many team records later broken by Gary Payton

WILKENS AT THE WHEEL

THE SUMMER OF 1977 WAS A TUMULTUOUS ONE FOR Seattle. Haywood, who had often clashed with Coach Russell, was traded away. Other players had also grown tired of Russell's domineering coaching style, so Schulman then forced Russell to resign. Without their star player and respected coach, the Sonics won just 5 of their first 22 games in 1977–78 with an interim coach before asking Lenny Wilkens back to coach in a permanent role.

Wilkens quickly reshaped Seattle's lineup, making Fred Brown the team's sixth man and inserting high-scoring guard Gus Williams into the starting lineup instead. Coach Wilkens also gave bigger roles to Marvin Webster—a 7-foot-1 center known as "The Human Eraser" for his shot-blocking skills—and rookie forward Jack Sikma. Finally, Wilkens started young point guard Dennis Johnson in place of Slick Watts.

SEATTLE SUPERSONICS

Fans called Gus Williams "The Wizard" due to his acrobatic moves and sharp shooting and passing

Lonnie Shelton's aggressive attitude made him a valuable scorer—and a league leader in fouls

Wilkens's "new" Sonics stunned the league by winning 42 of their final 60 games in the 1977–78 season, then roaring through the playoffs to reach the NBA Finals. "What did Wilkens have that Russell and Hopkins lacked?" asked Seattle sportswriter Blaine Johnson. "Maybe more organization, maybe more communication, [or] maybe he wound up with the right blend of personalities. One thing is certain—he put all the necessary ingredients into the pot at the right time."

In the Finals, Seattle faced off against the Washington Bullets, who were led by star center Wes Unseld. The series was an epic battle, but the Bullets won in seven games. Although disappointed, the Sonics vowed that they would be back, and they were. In fact, they faced off against the Bullets again in the 1979 NBA Finals. The Sonics weren't the same team, however.

Webster and Watts were gone, and Sikma had taken over as center. The forwards were Lonnie Shelton—the team's enforcer—and John Johnson. Williams and Dennis Johnson continued to form a magnificent guard duo, and Fred Brown and Paul Silas provided great bench support. Together, these players formed the "Seattle Seven," and they were unstoppable in the Finals. The Sonics destroyed the Bullets four games to one, bringing Seattle its first NBA championship.

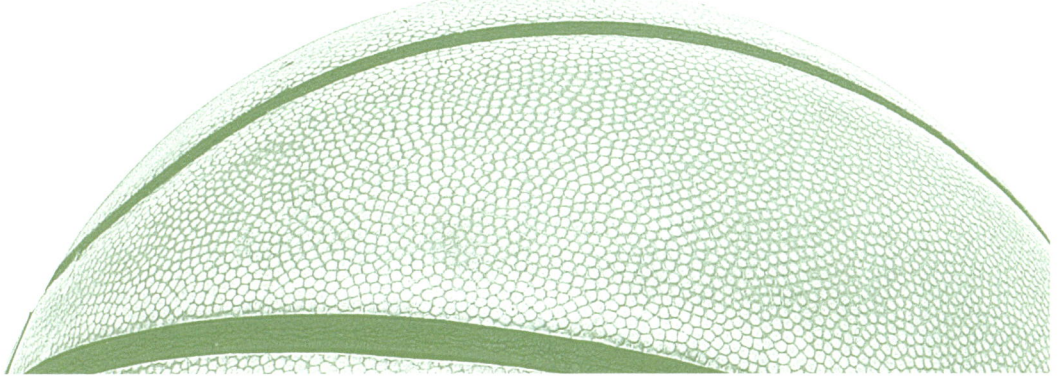

LENNY THE LEADER

Lenny Wilkens is probably the most successful player *and* coach in the history of the NBA. He made the Basketball Hall of Fame in both roles, and he led Seattle to its lone championship season in 1978–79, though some say the year before exemplified his finest coaching feat. Hired in November 1977, Wilkens took over a 5–17 team and spurred it to a 42–18 record the rest of the season and a trip to the NBA Finals, where Seattle lost in seven games. The next season though, Wilkens's Sonics were not to be denied. "This is what everybody wants," said Wilkens after the 1978–79 season. "You know how many guys come through this league and never even get involved in a championship?" By 2006, Wilkens had an NBA-record 1,332 wins as coach.

SEATTLE SUPERSONICS

By beating the Bullets in the 1979 NBA Finals, the Sonics won Seattle's first major pro sports championship

THE X-MAN MAKES HIS MARK

THE SONICS HAD REACHED THE PEAK OF THE BASKETBALL world, but they would not stay there. The Los Angeles Lakers rose to power, and many of Seattle's top players moved on. Jack Sikma, the last remaining member of the Seattle Seven, was finally traded away in 1986.

SEATTLE SUPERSONICS

Xavier McDaniel was famous for his rough-and-tumble defense and soft turnaround jump shot

An NBA iron man, star rebounder Michael Cage went eight straight seasons without missing a game

By that time, the Sonics were led by new coach Bernie Bickerstaff, who replaced Lenny Wilkens in 1985. Seattle soon featured a new collection of players as well. Xavier McDaniel, a skilled rebounder and head-shaven intimidator in the paint, led the way. "People always say [Chicago Bulls guard] Michael Jordan started the look, and I just laugh," said McDaniel of his trendsetting ways. "Actually I started the bald head. Slick Watts was the first guy in the NBA to do it, but he was long retired when I arrived. It became my trademark and then it became everyone's trademark, and I almost had to grow an afro back."

Along with "The X-Man," forward Tom Chambers impressed fans with his scoring and spectacular dunks. Guard Nate McMillan was the team's defensive stopper, while Dale Ellis gave the Sonics lethal three-point shooting, and 6-foot-10 forward Derrick McKey added versatility.

In 1988, Seattle added muscular power forward Michael Cage to its lineup and promptly posted its first winning record in four years. But, as had been the case throughout the decade, the Sonics found little success in the playoffs. The next two seasons, Seattle finished with 41–41 records and missed the playoffs.

MR. SONIC

When 6-foot-5 guard Nate McMillan was selected by the SuperSonics with the 30th overall pick in the 1986 NBA Draft, not many people took notice. And although he played for successful Sonics teams for the next 12 seasons, he garnered little fanfare. But make no mistake, "Mr. Sonic" was talented. He ranks in the top 10 in 10 different categories in the Sonics' record book and finished his career in 17th place on the all-time NBA steals list. He also holds the record for most assists by an NBA rookie in one game with 25, prompting his coach, Bernie Bickerstaff, to say, "Nate really gives us emotion. The players know that if they run the court and they're open, they will get the ball from Nate." McMillan coached the Sonics from 2001 to 2005.

REIGN MAN AND THE GLOVE

IN 1991–92, SEATTLE MADDENINGLY STARTED OFF 20–20, and Sonics fans wondered if their team would ever be better than average again. But then Seattle hired new head coach George Karl to guide rising Sonics stars Shawn Kemp and Gary Payton, and the Sonics began a new, winning era.

Kemp had jumped directly from high school to the NBA, joining the Sonics in 1989 at the age of 19. With his long arms and explosive vertical leap, "The Reign Man"—a pun on Seattle's rainy weather—thrilled local fans with an array of rim-rattling slams.

SEATTLE SUPERSONICS 25

High-flying forward Shawn Kemp earned a reputation as a dunking and shot-blocking extraordinaire

Gary Payton was the most feared defensive point guard of the '90s but could also score in bunches

Payton quickly earned a reputation around the league for two things: tenacious defense and trash-talking. He was quick, but he was also incredibly strong for his size. "The Glove" played suffocating defense and burned with intensity. Away from the court, however, Payton showed a softer side by creating his own charity—the Gary Payton Foundation—to help underprivileged children.

In 1993–94, the Sonics recorded an NBA-best 63–19 record. German forward Detlef Schrempf and sleepy-eyed forward Sam Perkins added veteran intelligence and excellent outside shooting, but the talented Payton-Kemp combination led the way. "They've always been the two young guys," said Coach Karl. "Now they've blossomed into perennial All-Stars."

Despite all their talent, the Sonics could never quite make it to the top. In 1995–96, the Sonics powered their way to a 64–18 record and the Western Conference title. Unfortunately, they then had to face the 72–10 Chicago Bulls in the NBA Finals. Although Seattle won two games, star guard Michael Jordan led Chicago to the championship.

SEATTLE NICKNAMES

Seattle has had a wealth of basketball players with colorful nicknames since the SuperSonics began operations in 1967. There was long-range shooting guard "Downtown" Freddie Brown and heady point guard Don "Slick" Watts in the 1970s. Intimidating forward Xavier "X-Man" McDaniel came to play in the '80s, and the '90s introduced Seattle fans to Shawn "Reign Man" Kemp, guard Hersey "Hawk" Hawkins, and forward Sam "Big Easy" Perkins. But one of the most skilled and appropriately nicknamed players the NBA has ever seen was "The Glove," Gary Payton. So nicknamed because he played such tight defense it seemed his man was actually *wearing* him like a glove, Payton made nine All-Star teams and eight straight appearances on the NBA's All-Defense first team, and won the NBA's Defensive Player of the Year award in 1996.

INTO THE NEW MILLENNIUM

IN 1997, SHAWN KEMP WAS TRADED AWAY FOR forward Vin Baker. Although Baker was not as spectacular an athlete as Kemp, he filled the Sonics' needs. "What we've got from Vin is more versatility, cleverness, backdoor lobs, and spins," said Coach Karl. "There's more variety."

Baker teamed up with Payton to lead the Sonics to another great record (61–21) in 1997–98. But then, despite having led the Sonics to seven straight winning seasons, Coach Karl was fired for his inability to bring home an NBA championship.

SEATTLE SUPERSONICS

Drafted in 1998, versatile forward Rashard Lewis (pictured) played alongside Vin Baker for four seasons

29

HOOPS

A smooth scorer and classy leader, Ray Allen led Seattle's offensive attack after Gary Payton's departure

NBA

The Sonics slumped until former player Nate McMillan took over as coach in 2001. McMillan relied on the veteran Payton to guide the Sonics on the court until Payton was suddenly traded to Milwaukee for shooting guard Ray Allen in 2003. The 2003–04 Sonics finished 40–42, their first losing record since 1986–87.

But in 2004–05, the Sonics bounced back, exceeding expectations with an impressive work ethic. Behind the play of the high-scoring Allen, explosive forward Rashard Lewis, locally grown point guard Luke Ridnour, and rebounding workhorse Reggie Evans, the Sonics won the Northwest Division with a surprising 50–32 record. In the playoffs, they beat the Sacramento Kings in the opening round before falling to the eventual champion San Antonio Spurs.

In a little more than 30 years, the Sonics have captured one NBA championship and the loyalty of the Pacific Northwest. With a franchise-ingrained tenacity made legendary by players such as Gary "The Glove" Payton, Sonics fans know their team will never lose due to a lack of effort. With a little luck and the right chemistry, Seattle will soon have a new title to go with the old.

MISPLACED STARS

When star players at the end of their careers switch teams, feathers can be ruffled. The 2000–01 season brought 38-year-old Patrick Ewing—who played center for the New York Knicks from 1985 to 2000—to the Sonics, angering Knicks fans. Then it was the Sonics fans' turn to get mad when 34-year-old Gary Payton was traded to the Milwaukee Bucks in 2003 after nearly 13 seasons in Sonics green and gold. One person who wasn't upset was George Karl, coach of the Bucks—and previously Payton's longtime coach in Seattle. "I said in Milwaukee that Gary Payton in another uniform makes me sad," Karl said. "It makes me pretty happy now." Payton later bounced from the Bucks to the Los Angeles Lakers to the Boston Celtics, while Ewing played one final season for the Orlando Magic.

INDEX

A

Allen, Ray **30**, 31

B

Baker, Vin 28
Basketball Hall of Fame 18
Beard, Butch 12
Bickerstaff, Bernie 23
Brown, Fred ("Downtown") 12, **13**, 14, 17, 27

C

Cage, Michael **22**, 23
Chambers, Tom 23

D

Defensive Player of the Year Award 27

E

Ellis, Dale 23
Evans, Reggie 31
Ewing, Patrick 31, **31**

H

Hawkins, Hersey ("Hawk") 27
Haywood, Spencer **10**, 11, 12, 14
Hazzard, Walt 11

J

Johnson, Dennis 14, 17
Johnson, John 17

K

Karl, George 24, 27, 28, 31
Kemp, Shawn ("The Reign Man") 24, **25**, 27, 28

L

Lewis, Rashard 31, **29**

M

McDaniel, Xavier ("The X-Man") **21**, 23, 27
McKey, Derrick 23
McMillan, Nate ("Mr. Sonic") 23, **23**, 31

N

NBA championship 17, 18
NBA Finals 17, 18, 27
NBA playoffs 12, 17, 18, 23, 27, 31
NBA records 18, 23

P

Payton, Gary ("The Glove") **4**, 5, 24, **26**, 27, 28, 31
Perkins, Sam ("Big Easy") 27, **27**

R

Ridnour, Luke 31
Rule, Bob 11
Russell, Bill 12, 14

S

Schrempf, Detlef 27
Schulman, Sam 12, 14
"Seattle Seven" 17, 20
Seattle SuperSonics
    first season 11
    name 8
Shelton, Lonnie **16**, 17
Sikma, Jack 14, 17, 20
Silas, Paul 17

W

Watts, Don ("Slick") 11, **11**, 12, 14, 17, 23, 27
Webster, Marvin ("The Human Eraser") 14, 17
Wilkens, Lenny 11, 12, 14, 17, 18, **18**, 23
Williams, Gus 14, **15**, 17